D1252708

CAT spies MOUSE

RINA A. Foti
and
DaVe Atze

WINDMILL
BOOKS ™

Published in 2020 by Windmill Books,
an Imprint of Rosen Publishing
29 East 21st Street, New York, NY 10010

Original edition published in 2018 by Big Sky Publishing

Typesetting: Think Productions
Cover Design: Dave Atze

Cataloging-in-Publication Data
Names: Foti, Rina A. | Atze, Dave.
Title: Cat spies mouse / Rina A. Foti and Dave Atze.
Description: New York : Windmill Books, 2020.
Identifiers: ISBN 9781725393707 (pbk.) | ISBN 9781725393721 (library bound) | ISBN 9781725393714 (6 pack)
Subjects: LCSH: Cats--Juvenile fiction. | Mice--Juvenile fiction. | Friendship--Juvenile fiction.
Classification: LCC PZ7.F685 Ca 2020 | DDC [E]--dc23

Manufactured in the United States of America

CPSIA Compliance Information: Batch BS19WM: For Further Information contact Rosen Publishing, New York, New York at 1-800-237-9932

In memory of my father,
Diego Musca, who continues
to inspire me.

4

Cat **spies** Mouse.

"I'm going to gobble you up, Mouse."

6

"Why would you do that?"

"Because *you're* a
mouse and *I'm* a cat
and that's that."

7

"So what?"

"So, that's the way it is."

"Well, that's not fair."

"Who cares
about fair?"

11

13

"It's not supposed
to be **nice**.
It's just the way it is!"

15

"But why, Cat?"

"I don't know *why*.
We can't be friends,
not now, not ever!"

"Don't say ever."

17

"Don't you get it?
You're a mouse and I'm a cat
and **that's that!**"

"Uh-oh!"

"What now, Mouse?"

18

"D-O-G"

"I'm going to **gobble** you up, Cat."

And guess what?

"That wasn't fair."

23

"Who cares about fair?
Dogs **hate** cats - everyone knows that."

"Well, that's not nice."

"It's not supposed to be **nice**.
It's just the way it is!"

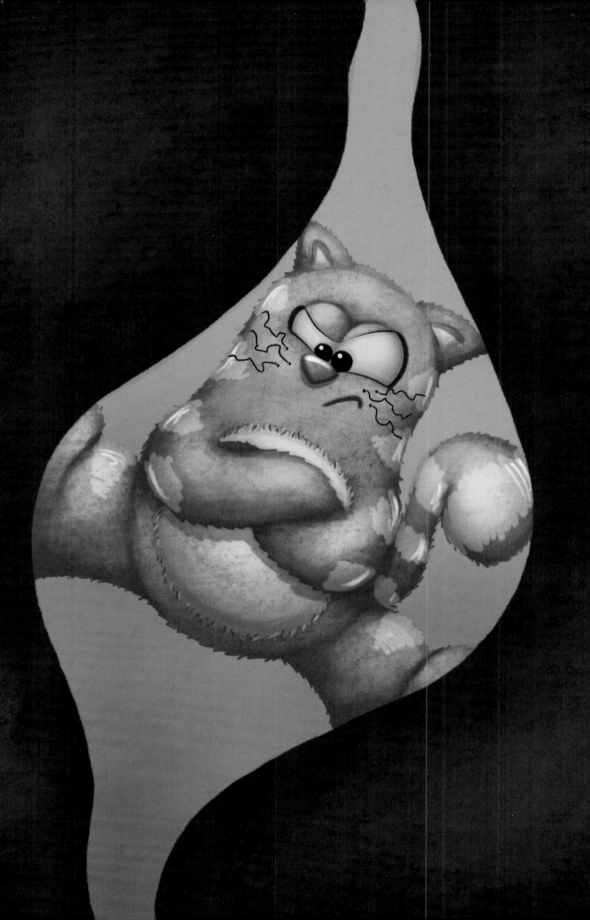

"But **why**, Dog?"

"I don't know **why!**"

"Think about it."

26

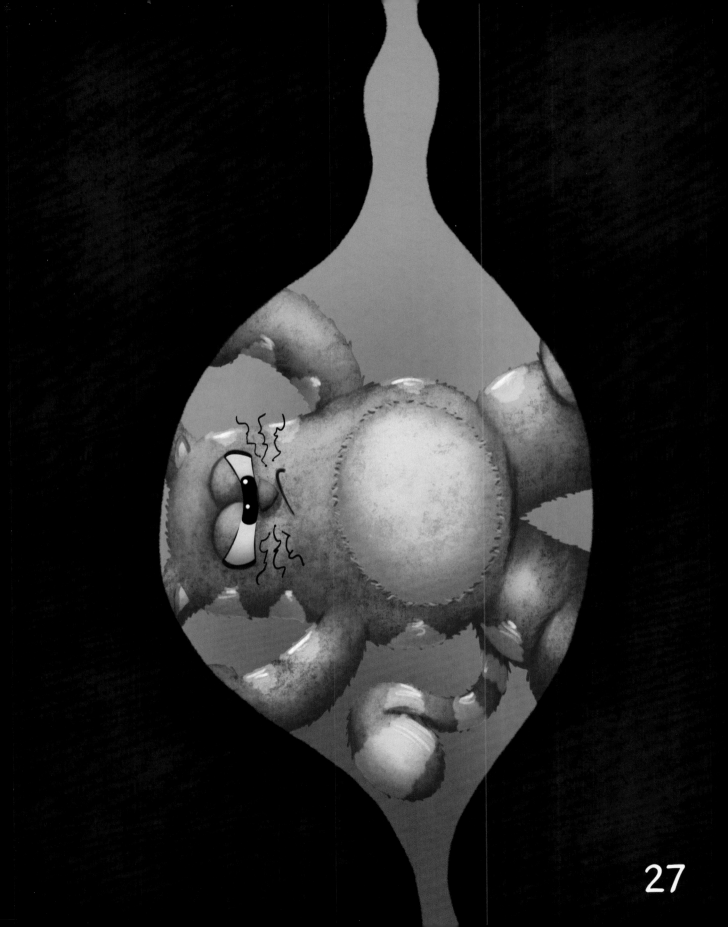

"I don't want to
think about it!"

"1, 2, 3,
3 and a half,
3 and three-quarters ..."

"Waah!"

"BURP!"

30

31

"Er ... um, Mouse, can we be friends?"